How to Love

Sally Edwards was born and grew up in rural Shropshire. The oldest of three daughters, she was introduced to the arts world at an early age, when she joined a singing group at her local church.

Sally's passion for music later led to her playing guitar and writing songs.

How to Love is Sally's first novel.

How to Love

A Novel

Sally Edwards

First published in Great Britain in 2015 by

Figtree Industries
3 Prospect Cottages
Snailbeach
Shrewsbury
SY5 0LR

1 3 5 7 9 8 6 4 2

A CIP catalogue record of this book is available from the British Library

This novel is entirely a work of fiction.
The characters and incidents portrayed in it are a work of the author's imagination.

ISBN 978-0-9572390-2-9

Designed and typeset in Garamond by Figtree Industries
Cover photograph by Ray Jacobs
Produced by Figtree Industries

How to Love

Chapter 1

On this early August morning, all is quiet around the tiny bungalow with its quaint little garden. The sun is shining and the birds are singing in the tall trees that form a beautiful backdrop. All is quiet ... until we step inside and hear the mayhem which erupted late last night and continues into breakfast time.

Charlie wakes up to the sound of her parents arguing and her mum crying out loud.

This is because Charlie finally 'did it'. After a year of staying silent and stressing over the reaction, three days before leaving for Brighton University, she came out as a lesbian to her parents. Charlie, thinking this was the biggest unkept secret on the planet, found the reaction quite a shock. After all, her bedroom walls are covered in posters of Shane from the L Word, KD Lang and Pink - not a male pop star in sight - plus her bedroom is constantly booming to the sound of Betty, Greymatter and KD Lang, and if you open her wardrobe, not a skirt, dress or anything remotely feminine can be found.

Charlie rubs her head and gives herself a light slap in the face to wake herself up before attempting to climb into her wheelchair. This isn't easy at the best of times, but today it is made even harder by the fact she dumped the chair in the most unreachable part of her room in her drunken state the night before. Yes, she came out to her parents after a heavy night with friends, celebrating her impending move to Brighton. As if moving hundreds of miles wasn't going to be hard enough for her over-protective parents to get to grips with, now they are not even speaking to her - just shouting at one another *about* her.

As Charlie sets to, fixing up her usual breakfast of black coffee and toast, the atmosphere changes to complete awkward silence. But every rattle of cutlery in the drawer and closing of cupboard doors is like a sledge hammer going at her head. Why did she agree to those Tequila Slammers when she was already seeing two of everything and everyone? She takes her first bite of toast and nearly throws it up over the kitchen table. She takes a tiny sip of coffee to wash it down. Everything is making her feel like she will die right here, but if this is the student way of life she is going to have to get used to it, so she stuffs the toast down her and makes a stronger coffee.

"We gonna have a chat about this, or are you just gonna give me the silent treatment?" says Charlie.

"Charlotte, your mother is very upset about last night, I think you owe her an apology."

Charlie giggles. "Upset about which part, Dad? That I came in drunk after a brilliant night out, or the fact I'm a Lesbian?"

"Charlotte!"

"Look, mum, I am really sorry I came back in such a state, but I am doing something really big and my friends mean a lot to me. They wanted to give me a good send off. I had a brilliant time and got home safely - you know they look after me. And I always thought you knew I was gay. I know I've never come out and said it, but I thought you knew. Is it so bad anyway? I'm still me; I've not changed; I just like girls, that's all."

"Do you realise how upset your Nan and Grandad would be if they knew? Bringing shame on the family like this!" Linda sobs again into the tea towel screwed up in her hands.

"Linda, steady on," says Dave.

"Shut up, Dave! I thought you were my husband? You are meant to support me in everything."

"Mum, don't be mean," snaps Charlie.

"Anyway, we can't discuss it now, we have to get ready."

Charlie looks up, confused.

"Your appointment, this afternoon," says Linda.

"Eh?"

"With Dr Rose, remember? Your final appointment with him before you become an adult. I've taken the day off to take you, remember?...pisshead!" laughs Dave.

"Yes, and when he smells your breath I'll be very surprised if he doesn't give you a lecture about looking after your kidneys. Someone's got to, lady," sneers Linda.

"In that case," says Charlie, "I'd better go get ready for the torture chamber. We can talk later."

Chapter 2

Charlie whizzes off to the shower and searches her wardrobe for something comfortable to wear; she knows these appointments normally involve lots of undressing and being poked and prodded from all angles, not in a good way either. On the upside, she remembers the fit looking nurse that works with Dr Rose and hopes she's still there.

Charlie spends ages on her look for the day and even longer looking for her iPod. The thought of listening to her mum boss her dad about the best way to go, fills her with dread, so having KD sing in her ears all the way to Liverpool seems a much better option.

As they hit the motorway and Charlie begins to recap on last night's argument and her behaviour, a wave of guilt hits her like a brick. She puts her hand in her pocket, about to listen to KD's silky smooth voice for the millionth time, and finds a polo mint pack, half eaten. She reaches over her mum's shoulder and offers her a polo.

"Peace offering? I am sorry mum, I did go too far and I did say some mean things to you. I know you love me, which is why this whole thing is so difficult. But you gotta understand, this isn't a choice, it's who I am, just as it's not my choice to be disabled. I am sorry, okay? But this I cannot change."

Reluctantly, Linda takes the polo. "Thank you. Dave, you want one?"

Dave takes a polo and moves the rear view mirror to wink at Charlie. "Thanks, Fonz," he says.

Fonz was the main character from Happy Days, a show Charlie watched as a kid, but her dad still insists on calling her that. Charlie remembers the time she went on a Riding for Disabled Association holiday to Cheshire. Her dad went on the final day, to help out, and was calling her Fonz. Weeks later, a member of the care team sent Charlie a postcard from Spain, addressed to Charlie Fonz; she actually thought this was Charlie's real surname ... the memory makes Charlie smile. She closes her eyes, turns up KD and drifts off to sleep, the hangover is still banging in her head and the smell of exhaust fumes is making her feel sick. She is sure her mum opened her window on purpose.

Chapter 3

Charlie sits quietly in the waiting room of the hospital, fidgeting with her clothes, her chair, anything to take away the boredom of the room, which hasn't changed in the eighteen years she's been visiting this place. It smells so clinical and is way too hot for her liking. She picks up a magazine that is two years out of date and throws it back on the table with a "tut". Her mum peers over her glasses, in Charlie's direction, with a look of disgust.

"Charlie Duke!" shouts a nurse.

"At long last," Charlie says, under her breath.

She wheels herself down the long, dark corridor with its photographs of different doctors and of the equipment which hospital engineers have invented over the years. There's one photo of a pair of blue callipers just being finished, that Charlie always says were hers. She wheels into the doctor's room with her mum and dad following behind, muttering to each other about god knows what.

"So, Charlotte, how are you?"

Charlie looks round the room in desperation. Where is the fit nurse?

Doctor Rose is flanked by the usual team of student doctors, nurses and specialists who just sit there staring and looking down their noses at her notes.

"Oh I'm fine, thank you, doctor, yes, no problems at all."

"And college is just around the corner. Are you excited?"

Charlie moves around in her chair, feeling very uncomfortable, still looking for the fit nurse.

"Yes, uni, next week I start. Can't wait. I will miss you though, doc, it's been a long time we have been meeting. But I will be a good girl, I promise."

She looks at him with that cheeky grin that everyone seemed to love when she was a kid. Doctor Rose looks up from his notes and laughs out loud.

"Oh, uni! I'm sorry, Madam. You still have that cheekiness, that charm, don't you? You who came into my room years ago, demanding sweets."

"That's why you love me, Doc, isn't it?"

"Do you have any questions, Charlie? Or do you, Mr and Mrs Duke?"

Linda smiles nervously and looks at the doctor. "Yes, can I ask about ... the future, you know, babies and things. Is it possible?"

At this question, Charlie goes bright red and sinks further into her chair, wishing the ground would swallow her up.

"Well, yes, that's a perfectly good question, and I see no reason why not. Many women with Spina Bifida have had children. Everything works the same in that regard, so that should definitely be possible, yes. Is that something you hope for, Charlie?"

Charlie smiles politely. "Maybe, I'm too young to think about that yet, though." She flashes her mum a look of annoyance.

"Sorry I'm late. Hello, Charlotte, how are you doing? So where are we at ?" Charlie smiles and blushes crimson as the hot nurse finally appears.

Chapter 4

Charlotte wakes up with a start and hears voices laughing and talking. Music bellows loudly from a radio and the smell of burnt toast wafts up her nostrils. She has been in Halls for a month and this is how she wakes up every morning.

She had to get here earlier than the others, so university facilities and access around the place could be sorted out before term started, so after a month it feels like she has been here forever. Whilst understanding the reasons, it was a lonely start to uni life and meant she left her mates back home earlier than normal.

She looks at her watch and quickly gets her things together for the shower, as she realises she's going to be late for her first psychology lecture. She's been told that Ms D. Winters is a force to be reckoned with for latecomers, especially on the first day of the course.

After her shower, she dresses and dashes to the communal kitchen to make breakfast. The place is a total tip: dishes piled up on the sink, crumbs everywhere, tea bags left on the side - she hates that. Why can't they just move another three feet and put those things in the bin? She curses under her breath and remembers family breakfasts - how much fun they were, how organised mum was in the kitchen, and how yummy dad's Sunday kippers smelled. Mum would cook them as a treat, ready for when dad got home from either football or golf, depending on the time of year. How she misses being spoiled!

She makes a mental note to have a word with the others about their laziness. She will refuse to live in a pig sty.

Charlie wheels over to the lecture hall and finds a spot to sit, but this new room seems very different to the others she has been in. The shelves are lower; there is a ramp up to the white board and there is no chair at the desk. She is used to the token changes the university makes for her specifically, but this room is a wheelchair user's paradise. Why? What is so special about this room?

Then the door opens and in wheels this middle-aged lady in the most expensive looking wheelchair Charlie has ever seen.

"Good morning, Class, please be seated. My name is Ms Delta Winters. Out there it's Ms Winters; in here you can call me Delta, but don't tell anyone, okay? I'm pretty relaxed about that kinda thing, but make me mad or disappoint me and it all kicks off. You understand?"

She looks around the room and smiles. "Listen, you be adults and work hard and I will respect you and do all I can to get you through this year, okay? But piss me off and I'll fail the lot of you. Good. Glad we got that straight."

So this is what all the fuss is about. She's American, a Yankee, and in a wheelchair. She has a rainbow key ring on her desk, so I'm guessing she's gay too? Charlie takes another good look. Just then, Delta looks up and spots Charlie looking at the key ring.

"Charlotte Duke, isn't it? Heard good things about you. Good grades, it seems, and a reputation for very high standards of work." She looks at Charlie expectantly.

"It's Charlie, actually."

"Okay, Charlie, it's nice to meet you. Listen, come by my office after classes, I may be able to give you heads up about some stuff to get you through uni, okay? Clubs, support groups and who to talk to about access issues. Say, around four thirty, room A10, down the hall?"

Delta smiles and Charlie looks deep into her eyes. OMG, is Delta flirting with me? She blushes, quickly picks up a pen and her note book and fiddles with the pages. Yup, she has to admit it, Ms Winters is HOT!!

On her way out of uni a notice board catches Charlie's eye. It is very colourful, with rainbow stickers all over it. She moves in to have a closer look: LGBT society recruitment meeting, 7pm tomorrow night, in room A10.

A voice says, "A good society to be involved with around here."

Charlie turns round quickly.

"Hi, sorry, didn't mean to make you jump. I'm Stella, a year two student. I'm in that society. If you are one of us, you should come check it out and meet some people. We have regular nights out, and debates, and charity events; it's brilliant, and Delta is always good fun - even lets us have parties at her place."

"Is that allowed?" Charlie enquires.

"No, not exactly, but, well, rules are made for breaking, from time to time."

"Sounds good. I need to get into the social scene around here; make new friends; find my feet, kinda thing, so this could be fun."

Stella smirks. "Sorry, you said find your feet, and

you are in a chair. It was kinda funny. Sorry, shouldn't laugh."

"He he, no worries, I'm cool with all that. I say go for a walk, etc. all the time. Don't be sorry. And, let's just say, on a night out, I like to get legless."

"Ha ha ha, legless, that's brilliant. You are okay, you know; I think you will get on with us lot. So ' you gonna come tomorrow night then? We go for a drink after the meeting, normally in town. It's not the best gay bar, but it's okay. Cheap drinks, music nights, and hundreds of lesbians; so what could be better?"

"Okay, we'll see how I feel after the meeting then, but it sounds good. What's the bar called?"

"The Unicorn."

Charlie turns around and heads down the corridor towards Delta's room, then turns to see Stella looking at her.

"See you later, speedy."

" Laters. They don't call me road runner for nothing. Meep meep."

Charlie eventually finds Delta's room, which isn't easy, as all the room numbers on the doors at uni are above her head.

"Hey, come in. You found me, then? Make yourself comfortable. You want some coffee? It's pretty rank; still can't get used to the Brits' idea of coffee, but what can I do? Twenty five years here and still complaining about the food, coffee and your god awful weather."

"So what brought you over here? A bit different from America, I guess?"

"A gal. Her family came to stay on my folks' ranch, when I was eighteen, and we fell in love. I moved here straight after college, and we were very happy for a long time, and, well, this is home now. I go back to see the family every year, but dad's too old to run the ranch now, so I will be going back this summer to help him sell up. Mum is in a home, with dementia, so … anyway, okay, so you are here, and gay, I take it, by the way I saw you looking at my key ring? You got a gal?"

"No, broke up few months before I came down here."

"So you are on the lookout? Plenty of us here, geez, we are everywhere these days, not like in my college years, when there was still a lot of homophobia around. It seems everyone is gay these days. Well, tomorrow's meeting will help you get to grips with what's happening around here - groups, events, that kinda thing. I let a select few come over to my place every now and then, for a get together. It's all on the quiet, you know, but hell, my place is accessible, obviously, so it would be okay for you. I'll let you know when the next gathering is. I do great food and some bring their guitars, etc. and we have a sing along. It's very chilled; you must come over."

"Okay, thanks, maybe, I don't know, maybe one night."

"It's okay, I don't bite, unless you want me to, that is. Ha ha ha."

Charlotte laughs nervously, then the conversation changes to access at the university, and additional support on offer.

"Did you understand your homework today?"

"Yeah, no problem. In by next Monday, right?"

"I can get you work extensions, if you need them."

"No, I'll be fine, well, on this one anyway. It will be handed in on time."

"Well, let me know if you change your mind, but I have big hopes for you, based on your report, so I'm looking forward to reading it. Anything else you wanna ask me?"

"Yeah. What happened ... to your partner?"

Delta looks down and her eyes fill with tears.

"Don't ask me about her again, please. She passed away four years ago - breast cancer. Now, if that's all, I need to go; I have meetings, then I need to get home. I have company tonight."

"Sorry - I mean about your partner - and for keeping you here too. Okay, see you next lesson, and thanks for the chat."

"See you at recruitment tomorrow night?"

"I'll be there - see ya later. And thanks again."

All the following day, Charlotte can't stop thinking about Delta. There is something not quite right. She seems very relaxed and almost too nice to be a lecturer at uni, and what is that overpowering herb-like smell that seemed to be all over her? Charlotte doesn't know for sure, but she has a notion that this is a cover up for the smell of weed. Yes, something very odd about Delta. But still, Charlie finds her strangely attractive for an older woman.

Chapter 5

Charlie edges into the room and spots Delta, who greets her and touches her hand.

"Come in, they don't bite. Everyone, this is Charlie, a first year student, one of my star students … I hope."

After about an hour, things become less formal. Charlotte is sitting next to the window, reading all the leaflets she's just been given, when Stella comes over.

"Hey, road runner, he he, you okay? We are heading over to the pub. Wanna join us? It's not the best for chairs probably, but we'll manage."

"Yeah, okay, could do with a drink actually. You sure you can manage? I don't want to be a pain."

"Yes, it's cool, there's plenty of us butch lesbians to get you in safely."

Charlie blushes a little and nods in approval.

A group of about six wander off down the street. This is Charlie's first real adventure around the city and she looks around with wide eyes, stopping occasionally to peer in shop windows. Within fifteen minutes, they arrive at the front door of a rather dull looking pub. The only colour on display is the giant rainbow flag draped from the bay window. Charlie notices a poster advertising: Live music on a Thursday night. Drinks half price before 9pm.

After negotiating with the bouncers about how best to get Charlie in - almost tipping her out as they try to lift her completely off the ground like some kind of Egyptian queen on her throne, they finally get to the bar and Charlie takes a good look around. The Unicorn is an old building, a bit worn-out, but the new owners have obviously done all they can to modernise.

There are posters of half naked women on the walls, t shirts for sale behind the bar, and the music played by the DJ is deafening. Charlie smiles as she looks at the talent on show, she could get to like this place.

The girls go ahead and find a tiny table in the annexe to sit at.

"Where are the loos?" Charlie asks.

"Just through there on the left, next to the pool room. Want me to come give you a hand? Not sure if the door is wide enough."

Charlie nods and Stella leads her down the narrow hallway, asking people to watch their backs as she ploughs through the crowd to a doorway.

"This is it. Go take a look, see what you think; we can go elsewhere if it's no good. We don't mind."

Stella opens the door to a room with two small sinks and another door at the far end which isn't wide enough to get a wheelchair through. This is the toilet. Charlie wheels herself right into the door.

"Shit, that's no good. Sorry, Charlie, shall we go?"

Charlie smiles with an 'I knew it' kind of look. She has become accustomed to places not having proper wheelchair access, toilets that were not built specially, those that the staff use as a store cupboard, or for which the magic key has been stolen. If you are lucky enough to get in, the bins, which have not been emptied by the cleaners, are often overflowing with used continence aids, cos, "well, not many people use this loo, so it gets forgotten about".

Under her breath Charlotte seethes at this thought, but smiling up at Stella, says: "No, it's okay, if you just close the first door and stop anyone else coming in, I can manage. It's fine, really."

Charlotte goes into the loo and manages to take a huge jump from chair to toilet, almost slipping as she lands, due to the toilet seat being broken. When she's finished, she realises the hand dryer on the wall is too high - naturally, so she shakes her hands and wipes them on her jeans, again seething under her breath.

She greets Stella, who is playing guard by the door, with: "Oh, that's better, I needed that."

"Manage okay, did you?"

"Yeah, fine, honestly, I've had to cope with worse than that, believe me, he he."

They make their way back to the table, where the others are getting well and truly drunk and messing around. The atmosphere has changed in The Unicorn and Charlie sees that a singer is setting up ready to perform. The DJ has stopped and everyone has quietened down a little.

"Do you know the singer then, or is she just some random?"

"No, that's Hannah Macey; she's local. She sings in here at least once a month."

Charlie smiles in acknowledgement and takes a closer look at the tall, slim, tattooed singer with jet black hair and massive boobs, wearing tight jeans, a t shirt and a waistcoat. Charlie's eyes nearly pop out and she can't hold in a smile.

"I know, isn't she gorgeous, all the ladies love her. Wait till you hear her voice too," says Stella. "OMG, she's lush. She's in a band, but does a lot of solo gigs in Brighton. She's from here, so I guess it's good for her to come for some gig practice."

The evening goes by so quickly for Charlie; lots of laughing, drinking games, and lots of hot ladies checking her out. She is in heaven. About half way through the evening, a group of girls comes in giggling and generally seeming excited. Then, the door opens again and in walks this tall, athletic looking woman, with tattoos and hair in a quiff. Brimming with confidence, she says hello to different women as she makes her way to the bar, kissing one or two on the cheek.

Charlie taps Stella on the shoulder and gestures with her head towards this gorgeous woman standing at the bar with hordes of women vying for her attention and offering her drinks.

"Oh, that's Maria, Maria Da Rossi, She owns Costello's Italian place on the high street. Every lesbian in this bar wants to get her into bed, and she knows it. Proper cocky fit though; I certainly wouldn't kick her out of bed myself. But I wouldn't wanna be her girlfriend; I'd be too jealous of all the other women. There's no way someone like her can be faithful, so I wouldn't go anywhere near her. But nice to look at.

Charlie, you have gone redder than a letter box, are you okay?"

"Yeah, of course, silly, I'm fine. Sorry, must have zoned out for a second. Where were we?"

Charlie allows herself one last glance over Stella's shoulder towards the bar, where Maria stands drinking a beer. Mid glance, Maria turns round and looks straight at Charlie, smiles, raises her pint and mouths "Hi." Charlie smiles back and there it is: Bang! She looks into the most beautiful sparkling blue eyes she has ever seen. She had no idea you could get eyes that blue. She feels her stomach do a somersault. Wow, this woman is beautiful!"

Charlie hears the line being sung: "It's not the same when I look in your eyes," and realises she is now staring at Maria like a child staring at its presents on Christmas morning. She adjusts herself in her chair and takes a drink. The group carry on chatting and enjoying the music for a while, then Charlie feels the presence of someone near her. Stella and the others go quiet and smile at Charlie.

"Hiya, ladies, how are you? Are you having a good night?"

"Hi, Maria, how you doing? Not seen you for a while. Night off, is it?" giggles Stella.

"Yeah, I've just taken on a new chef, part time, to give me some extra time off. Not too sure if he will work out, but I'm giving him a month's trial. So who's your friend? Not seen you before. I'm Maria Da Rossi, and you are?"

"I'm Charlie, Charlie Duke. It's my first night in here. Studying at the uni down the road."

Maria offers Charlie a hand and Charlie holds out hers, thinking they will shake hands. Maria takes Charlie's hand, kisses it gently, looks into her eyes and says, "Pleasure to meet you, hun."

Charlie goes so red now, the girls start to giggle.

"I've got a new menu starting on Saturday night. Why don't you come in, say around eight, and sample it? All half price, and drinks free! Special one night offer for students, and I will book you a nice table on the ground level, near the bar. I have just updated the bathrooms too, and there is a disabled loo."

" Meals half price, was that?" questions Charlie.

"And drinks on the house all night, just for your table. So shall I book it for you?" Maria looks round the table for an answer.

"Yes, go on then, a nice meal and free drink. We'd be mad to say no, eh, girls?" Charlie's eyes appeal for Stella to help her out.

"Great, that's settled then," Maria says. "Oh, one thing, I better take a phone number from one of you, just in case there are problems. Don't want to disappoint you." She looks in Charlie's direction.

"Here, take mine. These lot are so pissed they probably can't remember their own numbers."

"Speak for yourself, Charlie, how many shots you had? You will need help into bed at this rate, hehehe."

Maria gets her phone out of her jeans pocket and keys in Charlie's number. After buying the girls a round, she goes and sits at the corner of the bar, chatting to the bar staff and generally looking cool.

The bell rings for last orders and there's a stampede to the bar. Charlie is just beginning to think she might regret all this tomorrow, when Delta glides into the bar and sees the group. She comes over and starts chatting.

"How are you managing in Halls, Charlie? You coping okay?"

"Well, it's not the best, to be honest," admits Charlie, "but I'm managing - just about."

"I've had an idea. I have a friend who owns some student digs in town. She's coming to my place for dinner tomorrow; why don't you come over, so I can introduce you? I think she's just bought a bungalow - might be worth checking out."

"Oh, really? That does sound good. Okay, I'll come by your office tomorrow, and get your address."

"Make sure she gets into bed, okay, ladies? She's a bit fluffy I think. Hehehe."

"We will, Delta, don't worry, you have a good night."

Delta melts into the crowd around the bar and Stella stands up.

"Right, well I've got an early start tomorrow, so I'd better go. Are you lot going clubbing, or are you coming back?"

"You mind if I come back with you, Stella? The room's spinning. I don't think clubbing is a good idea tonight."

"Come on, road runner, let's get you home. And no puking in people's gardens along the way! Okay?"

"Can't promise anything. Just don't take me past any food places and I'll be fine. Meep meep, let's go!"

Charlie bundles her way through the crowd, to the front door of The Unicorn, before Stella and the other girls have had time to gather their belongings. She looks for a bouncer to help. Just then, she gets a tap on the shoulder. Maria is behind Charlie's chair, looking angry.

"Here, hold on tight, I can do this on my own. Why does it take two men to do the simplest of things, for god's sake. You hold my pint, and don't spill it, okay? Or you are buying me another. Hehehe."

"What, me? Spill beer? I'd rather lose an arm; don't worry. You ever done this before?"

"Nope, but I'm a fast learner." Maria is calmer now. "What's the best way to get you down?"

The bouncer arrives and argues with Maria, over Charlie's head, about the best way to get her out of the bar. Eventually, Maria wins the argument and helps Charlie out of the doorway, almost landing her on the lap of a woman sprawled on the ground, drunk and giggling.

"Thought I was getting lucky, then," says Charlie. Maria laughs.

"I'll sit on ya lap any time, darling," says the woman. " - give you a lap dance. How's that?"

"Yeah, okay, darlin'." Charlie nudges Maria. "Gotta catch me as I run the other way, though, ya dog."

"Ooh, bitchy," says Maria.

"Well, people like her do my head in."

"No thought for anyone but themselves, people like that. Must annoy you sometimes, hun?" says Maria.

"Naaa, you just have to take it with a pinch of salt and walk away. They only say things cos they are uncomfortable. They don't realise they are patronising you. I can normally laugh my way out of comments like that, but occasionally I get a pat on the head, which really pisses me off. I'm eighteen, for fuck's sake, not eight. Grrrr - breathe, Charlotte," she says.

Maria kneels down to Charlie's eye line and places a hand on hers: "She didn't hurt you, did she? I'll go have a few words, if you want?"

"No, I'm fine, honestly, that's nothing. I can tell you a few tales of funny things that have happened to me on a night out. But thank you, and thanks for the help at the door."

Maria stands up and squeezes Charlie's shoulder. "You're welcome, hun. I'd like to hear some of those stories, sometime."

"Well, you have my number. I finish classes around half four, most days, so ..." Charlie looks deeply into those baby blue eyes again, and is almost paralysed by desire.

Maria gives her shoulder another squeeze and says, "See you Saturday, Charlie."

Just then, Stella and the other girls stumble out of The Unicorn singing "I am what I am," loudly.

Blowing a kiss to Charlie, Maria walks over to Stella, says something, turns to face Charlie again and waves.

Stella and the others come rushing over to Charlie.

"You all right, road runner?" Gently, but in a drunken fashion, they get her back to Halls and help her to bed, leaving a bowl and glass of water nearby - just in case.

Chapter 6

Charlie sits in the back of the taxi on her way to Delta's place.

When she bumped into her at lunchtime, by the disabled loo at uni, Delta gave her a piece of paper and said, "And don't be late; dinner will go cold otherwise. Hehehe."

The driver helps Charlie out of the back of the taxi. As she pays the fare, she looks over to the house and sees the door opening. Charlie pushes herself up to the door and sees Delta sitting there, grinning, wearing very different clothes from those she wears at uni: jeans and a rugby shirt, or is it an American football shirt?

"Perfect timing; I've just opened a bottle of wine. Come in, out of the cold."

Charlie enters the house and can't help but look at every detail as she goes from hallway to living room. It is a modernised Victorian terrace, with a mixture of old and modern decor: tiled floor in the narrow hallway, roses around the ceiling lights, wooden floors throughout, downstairs, with a full length mirror on the wall opposite the front door. A stairlift at the bottom of the stairs is folded neatly, covered up almost completely by a pile of winter coats hanging from the banister.

"Just put your coat on top of the others on the banister, honey; they will probably fall down at some point, but hey, better they are on the floor than outa reach, right?" says Delta.

Charlie becomes aware of the smell of food wafting through the house. It smells like roast beef, yeah, like mum makes on Sundays, with all the trimmings, and apple crumble for pudding. Would she be having apple crumble tonight? Charlie smiles to herself as she finds her way to the living room. Delta is pouring a drink from a wine bottle - there is that herb smell again, too. Sitting on the sofa, leaning forward, reaching for her drink, is a woman in her mid fifties, smartly dressed in a trouser suit. She stands up and reaches over to shake Charlie's hand.

"You must be Charlie. I'm Brenda Reed. Nice to meet you."

"Hello. Nice to meet you. Yes, I'm Charlie." Charlie feels a bit intimidated by Brenda, with whom, it seems, Charlie will have nothing in common. Brenda is obviously well to do, and a businesswoman.

"Brenda and I first met when I moved over here with Krysta. We were neighbours for, ooh, eight years or more. Is that about right, Brenda?"

"Sure is, honey," says Brenda. "Don't be fooled by my dress code; I've been to the estate agent's today, signed all the paperwork and got the keys to another property, so I'm kinda celebrating."

"She's bought that bungalow I was telling you about, Charlie, so I thought you two had better meet and see if it would be okay for you," says Delta. Don't be fooled by the suit; she isn't all that smart ya know. She's actually a jack-of-all-trades."

"And definitely master of none. Hehehe, yup, that's me," says Brenda.

Charlie laughs along with them, nervously. She finds a spot in the corner of the room, to sit, a perfect place to have another good look around the living room. The roaring open fire spits out sparks on the marble surround, making Charlie jump each time. There is very little furniture apart from a two seater sofa, a cabinet filled with books, and photos on the fireplace and hanging from the walls. The dining table is small, but makes eating very cosy, and is at the perfect height for Charlie. She is often faced with tables too high, needing to put an extra cushion or coat underneath her. It all seems very English, until Charlie spots a photograph on the fireplace, of Delta, another woman, and Ronald Reagan.

"Yeah, that's me and Krysta, with Reagan, at The Whitehouse. We went to a charity thing with her work, one night. Good times."

Charlie looks at the photograph again, in amazement. "Wow, what was he like? I've never met anyone famous before?"

"I couldn't really get to speak to him properly; too many other more important folk there for him to suck up to, for votes. So, Brenda, tell us about this bungalow."

The next while is spent with Brenda telling the others about this modern build bungalow she has just bought, and how she intends to rent it out. They all agree to make a date to view it, with the idea that if Charlie is happy she may move in.

Anything has got to be better than living in Halls. Things have been going from bad to worse there, with people up all hours, drunk, shouting, playing loud music and arguing. And the mess in the kitchen is getting worse too. If this bungalow seems right, Charlie decides she will definitely be moving in, as her sleep is vital and she is so drained from endless sleepless nights.

It will be more accessible in the bathroom of the bungalow; much better than the old mouldy shower seat, grimy tiles on the walls and fag butts on the window sill. The bathroom in Halls hasn't been decorated or updated in over ten years, judging by the state of it, and the heating is dodgy, to say the least. Each night, Charlie turns out the light and sees her breath in the air. Yes, a new warm, accessible bungalow seems the perfect solution. And it is just around the corner from The Unicorn.

Charlie can feel herself falling asleep by about ten thirty. She is full from dinner and very hot from sitting next to the fire all night. She asks Delta for a taxi number and rings for a cab.

" - be here in ten minutes, they said."

" - be more like twenty-five, if the truth be known," says Delta.

Charlie makes a visit to the toilet and soon enough the cab arrives, beeping its horn, which sets the entire neighbourhood's dogs off, barking.

"Thanks for a great time, Delta. Nice to meet you, Brenda. I've almost finished that assignment. It will be on time," says Charlie, smiling at Delta.

"So long, honey, take care," says Delta, as she sits in the doorway, waving. Did Charlie just see Brenda's hand on Delta's shoulder? What is going on between those two? Charlie wonders.

Chapter 7

Before Charlie has really had time to think, it is Saturday morning: the day of the meal at Maria's place. This fills her with both excitement and dread. She hasn't been on a date in ages, and she takes at least two hours to make up her mind what she is going to wear. She decides on smart: black trousers, a white shirt, and a black and white pin striped jacket. She almost cancels at one point, too nervous to go. The girls will probably tease her all night. Eventually, though, she talks herself round, and starts getting ready at six o'clock. She sprays so much perfume on, you can smell where she has been from two hundred yards down the road.

At the restaurant, they all sit down at the best table in the house and start to view the menu, with great excitement. The closest that most of the girls have come to eating in a restaurant, is a sit down on a Saturday afternoon, at McDonald's.

"Should we order a bottle of wine, Charlie?" says Stella.

"When in Rome - as they say," replies Charlie. Everyone at the table bursts into laughter. As they quieten down, the kitchen door opens. Dressed in an Armani suit, looking proudly at the busy tables, is Maria. Charlie spots her instantly, and starts to feel her stomach do flips so badly she thinks she will either pass out or be sick.

"Calm down, woman, you'll do yourself a mischief," says Stella, in Charlie's ear.

"Be cool, calm and collected, yeah?" replies Charlie. Stella nods in approval.

The night goes by, but Charlie hardly eats a thing off her plate, too excited to even think of eating.

What is she going to use as an excuse? She can't say there is something wrong with the food, can she? The restaurant fills up and gets noisy, but, eventually, their table is the only one left to be cleared. They have been there the whole evening. The waiters take the dessert dishes and coffee cups away, and Maria comes over to ask if everything has been to their satisfaction.

They all make polite conversation, then Stella says, "We should order a taxi back for you, Charlie."

Maria looks puzzled.

"Oh, I'm going back to Halls. These lot are going clubbing, but I have an essay that needs finishing so I'm getting an early night and getting on with it, first thing," Charlie explains.

"Well don't ring the normal rabble; they are not very polite. I know a firm that has taxis with ramps, which I'm assuming would be better for you, Charlie?"

"If you're sure you don't mind? Thanks, Maria." Charlie smiles, and blushes at the sight of Maria definitely checking her out.

"No trouble at all," says Maria.

Maria disappears into a back room and closes the door. The girls say their goodbyes as they see their cab pull up outside.

" - You sure you will be okay, Charlie? I don't mind waiting for you, just to make sure you get back," Stella offers.

"Don't worry, I will look after her," says a voice from behind them. Maria is standing there and Charlie is surprised to see her looking nervous. "The taxi will be here in about fifteen minutes, okay?"

Stella walks out of the door, waving; she mimes "Call me" to Charlie and blows her a kiss.

"Why don't you come into the office, where it's warmer? I have to turn the lights off in here, in case I get an idiot trying to book a table at stupid o'clock."

They move into the office and Maria shifts a few things out of the way to make more room for Charlie.

"Not the best space for a wheelchair - sorry," says Maria, still looking nervous.

"I'm sure I can manage," says Charlie, feeling more

confident in Maria's presence now the others have gone and there is no one to tease her.

Maria sits on the office chair, pours a scotch and hands one to Charlie. "I bet you can," she says, moving in so close that Charlie can feel her breath on her nose. Charlie looks into those gorgeous bright blue eyes and her stomach flips.

Maria puts down her drink and places her hand on Charlie's face. Gently holding her chin in her hand she kisses her softly and passionately. She pauses for a second to see Charlie's reaction and Charlie reaches out and pulls her in closer.

Maria stands up and takes off her jacket, then slowly takes off Charlie's jacket.

"Is this okay?" she whispers.

"Just come and sit here. It will be fine," says Charlie, tapping her lap. Maria carefully sits down on Charlie's lap as if riding a bicycle, a leg draped over each wheel. Charlie continues to kiss Maria as she removes the shirt from her athletic torso, her perfume wafting into the air, making Charlie feel dizzy with desire. It is Calvin Klein, Euphoria: Charlie's favourite.

Charlie continues to explore Maria's body; she can't believe how fit she is. She traces each tattoo with one finger, provocatively, feeling every muscle in Maria's biceps and shoulders as she does so.

"Is it safe to pick you up?" whispers Maria.

Charlie looks confused, then turns to see a leather sofa in the corner of the room.

"I'm sure, with a body like that, you can lift me just fine," she says, winking at Maria.

Maria stands up and Charlie shows her the best way to lift her, one hand behind her back, the other under her legs. Maria does this with such care, never taking her eyes off Charlie. She kneels down on the side of the sofa, gently placing Charlie on her back.

Soon, both are completely naked, and Maria carefully strokes Charlie's breasts and plays with the nipples, kissing them and teasing them with her tongue. She places passionate kisses all over Charlie's body, then slides one hand up her thigh and between Charlie's legs. Her fingers quickly find the G spot; Charlie takes a deep breath with excitement and lets out a loud moan, her kisses becoming more passionate as she asks for more. Charlie places her legs around Maria's waist like a tightening vice, with cries of desire, and feels a warm, wet sensation between her legs. With this, Maria penetrates a little faster with her fingers and tongue, looking at Charlie as if to ask if it is too much. Charlie grabs Maria's head, demanding more.

After a while the penetration becomes slower and more gentle and Maria repeats the kissing of every inch of Charlie's body, teasing the skin with her lips and tongue until eventually her kisses find their way back to Charlie's lips. They kiss passionately and playfully again and lie in an embrace, breathing as one, sweat pouring from them both.

Maria looks up and says, "Are you okay?"

Charlie nods and smiles: "There never was a taxi, was there?"

"How did you guess?" says Maria.

"Cos if there was one, they would have been beeping their horn for the last hour and got fed up and gone by now, anyway."

They squeeze each other and laugh out loud.

"My place is only round the back of the restaurant. If you want to stay, I can help you with whatever you need."

Charlie looks worried.

"It's okay, I will have your nose back into your essay before ten," says Maria.

"If you're sure it's okay. Can you manage? I don't want to make life difficult for you - with having to move things, you know?" Charlie says.

"It's fine; we can manage." Maria places one more passionate kiss onto Charlie's lips, before standing up from the sofa and beginning to get dressed. She hands Charlie her clothes. "Make sure you put your jacket on; I don't want you getting a cold; it's freezing out."

"You sound just like my mum," Charlie laughs.

Maria helps Charlie into her wheelchair and they leave the building through a door at the back of the office. Maria locks up and shows Charlie the way to the house.

Chapter 8

"For fuck's sake, why doesn't this make any sense?" shouts Charlie, at her book.

She's read the same paragraph at least six times and can't remember a single word. This isn't down to her not understanding the content, but more to do with the fact that it is Sunday evening and she hasn't heard a word from Maria since last night's passionate encounter. Is she being too hasty, or is Maria this player that Stella and everyone else warned her about? Charlie isn't used to being messed around; she only ever had one girlfriend at home, and that was all good, until Charlie decided to end it because of going to uni.

At two a.m. she texts Stella: Finally got something written down. May have to ask for an extension though - not sure Delta will be satisfied. Still no word from M. What a bitch … Gutted! Meep meep, see you in class xx

All night Charlie tosses and turns, thinking about what happened on Saturday. She can't help but think the worst. Is Maria really the love em and leave em kind? Was Charlie a "pity fuck"? Or was she the brunt of some childish bet? Lots of times, at school, boys would come up and kiss her, for a bet with their mates, just so they could say they kissed a disabled kid -
But surely not this time? Not Maria. Not the way she kept looking at me in the pub that night. And her concern when I fell out the doorway ...

Eventually, Charlie falls asleep, not sure whether to be angry or cry.

She does manage to get to class the next day. After a bit of one-to-one advice, Delta agrees to a week's extension on the essay - Charlie lies that she had problems with her laptop which delayed her finishing it properly.

On leaving class, Delta says, "Say, what are you doing Friday night? I'm going to a jazz club in town. You would not believe who the star performer is!"

Friday night comes around and still no word from Maria. By now, Charlie is furious, and determined to get her out of her head, she rings Stella and arranges to meet her in The Unicorn later that night, as she doesn't think for one minute she will enjoy the jazz club.

"I mean, come on," she says, on the phone to Stella, "who our age likes jazz? It's old people's music. But Delta seems to think I will enjoy it, so I may as well go for an hour."

She meets Delta at seven thirty p.m., outside what looks like an old run down cinema, and she can't believe her eyes. The men look very odd and the women looked even odder. Then, she catches a glimpse of a smartly dressed man, holding a saxophone, staring right at her and Delta. He comes over to them, kisses Delta on the cheek and says, "Well, she actually got you here."

Charlie is puzzled. More so, when the man comes in to kiss her on the cheek. It is then she realises the 'man' is Brenda, from the night at Delta's house. She is a sax playing drag king! OMG, this all makes sense, now. This is some kind of drag night venue. Should be interesting, she thinks.

They exchange a few words, then make their way to the front table by the small staged area. The music speaker is right by Charlie's head and is very loud, but she is thankful for a decent spot from where she can see what is happening onstage. So often, she has been to festivals and gigs where she either had to sit right at the back, only ever hearing the performances, and seeing the backsides of the people in front of her; or else she was placed right at the front, by the bouncers and the massive speakers. Her mates back home joke that, at a pride event, this is very lucky because she gets the best view of all the women's backsides. In reality, neither back nor front is ideal; it is just another access issue Charlie faces with a positive attitude, but secretly hates.

The first few acts come and go, and Charlie is struggling to hide her boredom. But then the compère comes on stage.

"And now, ladies and gentle folk, I give you all what you have been waiting for - Mr BB Reed!"

The audience gives a massive round of applause. There is shouting, stomping of feet and whistling; then onto the stage, like some kind of king arriving to address his people, walks Brenda!

The first half of Brenda's performance comes to an end and the compère announces a fifteen minute interval.

Delta leans over to Charlie and says, "I just gotta go backstage; Brenda's got something for me. I need something to calm down these goddamn shakes tonight." Sure enough, Charlie notices Delta's right leg shaking violently. Then Delta zooms off as if she is on a mission.

Delta returns about ten minutes later. She looks much more relaxed and her leg has stopped dancing. She has obviously been outside as Charlie can smell the cold on her ... and that herb again. Yes, this convinces Charlie, Delta smokes weed and Brenda is her supplier.

After the show, Charlie and Delta sit outside waiting for taxis. It is freezing and Charlie needs a proper drink. She texts Stella and suggests they meet outside Monty's - a gay club in town. The two women chat about Brenda's performance, and then Delta leans over and offers Charlie a drag on the joint she is obviously enjoying.

"Go on, it might help the tension in your back."

Charlie looks surprised.

"I can tell by the way you're sitting, you've got back pain. Right?"

"Yeah, I have," Charlie admits. She leans over and takes the joint from Delta's hand.

"Just go steady, okay?" Delta advises.

The taxi arrives for Charlie and she speeds off to the club, where the others greet her. Charlie tells them all about the experience at the drag club: the bad acts, but also how good Brenda was. When she shares the information about the weed, no-one seems surprised.

"Oh, we all know about that; she smokes like a chimney at her parties. We have had some brilliant nights there. It's meant to help her MS, but If she got caught she'd lose her job," explains Stella.

The girls enjoy a good dance, and Charlie feels better about the Maria thing at last. On their way out of the club, Charlie says "I'm starving. Fancy some chips, girls?"

They all agree this is the best idea of the night. They head across the road to the chip shop. Charlie stays outside, as it's a tiny shop with an awkward step. At this point, Charlie begins to feel a bit unwell; the place is spinning and faces are becoming blurred. She hears voices talking in the background but can't recognise who they belong to. Confused, she finds herself in a quiet spot, away from the club; it is cold and dark and the voices are still there, but still she can make no sense of it. The vision she has feels very weird: things seem to be upside down. What the hell did Delta give her earlier? This isn't right. Then she hears voices again.

"Tell you what you lot need; a real man, that's what you lot need. You don't know what you're missing. Now keep quiet and stay still."

Charlie feels something heavy leaning on her body. She smells beer and hears the sound of fabric tearing, then the lights go out.

Chapter 9

Charlie wakes up to a bright light shining in her face, she panics and shoots up from the hospital bed, demanding to know what is happening.

The doctor catches her by the arm and says, "It's okay, Charlotte, you're in hospital. Calm down, you are going to be okay."

The doctor goes onto explain that her friends found her, unconscious, behind the chip shop, and they dialled 999. She had been mugged, and they want to examine her to establish whether she has been sexually assaulted. At this point, Charlie notices two police officers waiting outside the room.

As the doctor continues to explain events, memories flash into Charlie's mind: feeling unwell, the strange voices, blurred vision and the smell of stale beer. Charlie tries to sit up and a massive pain rips through her, from her head, down the length of her back, and she tastes stale beer. She wants to brush her teeth but how can she? She feels so alone.

At this thought, she begins to cry, and the doctor says softly, "I can delay the police from talking to you for a little longer. Your friend is here; she is desperate to see you. Shall I let her in?"

Charlie looked towards the door and there stands Stella with her arms full of Charlie's belongings and a bunch of flowers.

The two friends chat for a while and Stella sobs as she explains how guilty she feels for leaving Charlie alone. They clear the air and hug each other.

"I can't believe someone can do that to a disabled woman; it's disgusting, road runner. I'm so sorry. I'd like to get a knife to his throat. Picking on someone for being gay is bad enough, but a disabled person? That's the lowest of the low."

The doctor comes back to say Charlie needs some rest before her examination. There is a lot of bruising on her upper legs, so they want to make sure she hasn't been raped.

Stella leaves, still sobbing, promising to be back tomorrow.

An hour or so later, the examination is over, and to Charlie's relief there is no evidence she has been raped. Maybe someone disturbed the guy before he went that far. The nurse gives her a tablet for the pain and another to make her sleep. She swallows them gladly and settles down. She begins to drift towards sleep, listening to the hustle and bustle of the ward, but just as she is dropping off she becomes aware of a figure standing over her bed. Charlie comes to, rubbing her eyes to take a better look.

" I can't take my eyes off you for two minutes and you're in trouble. How are you feeling, babe?"

Charlie isn't sure whether to be delighted or furious to see Maria.

"Oh, so now you decide to appear!" she snaps.

Maria is clearly taken aback; unused to women standing up for themselves. She apologises, saying that no one had ever got into her head as much as Charlie. She explains she was called away on family business, suddenly, but on her return saw one of the girls from Charlie's class in the market who told her what had happened.

"If you need somewhere to stay, to recover, I'm sure we can manage at my place."

Charlie declines the offer, saying she will be better off getting on with things in her own way. She wants nothing more than to jump into Maria's arms and hide away, but doesn't want Maria to think she is under the thumb. If Charlie's affection is worth anything to Maria, she is going to have to fight for it.

After some small talk about the weather and how business is picking up at the restaurant, Maria leans into Charlie's face and says, "If you need anything at all, you just call me, okay?" She gazes into Charlie's eyes and smiles, expecting a kiss.

"Thanks. I will be okay though. I may come over for another meal with the girls soon - we enjoyed the food." Charlie places a quick peck on Maria's cheek. Maria looks to the floor, sad, even lost.

For a split second, Charlie feels sorry for her, but then remembers she is still angry. Maria could have called to say she was away, but no, she just disappeared.

"See you later, Maria. Thanks for visiting me."

Later that night, Charlie lies in the hospital bed, trying to sleep, but her head is spinning so fast with thoughts and emotions, she thinks she will fall off the bed. She has told the doctor not to contact her parents, but right now she really needs a cuddle from her mum. She is in pain, feels angry with 'that man', and is worried about falling behind at uni if she needs to take time off. But most of all, she needs those strong tattooed arms to hold her, and wants to stare into those beautiful blue eyes. She needs to hear the words "I'll look after you" come from Maria's lips. Oh, those lips, she thinks, which finally makes her smile. With a warmer, calmer feeling now, she drifts off to sleep, pretending Maria is holding her ... Yes, this is it, she thinks: I am in love!

Chapter 10

"I'm so glad term's nearly over; I need a break," declares Stella. "It's been a tough few weeks for you as well, Charlie. How are you feeling?"

"Physically, I'm lots better, and thanks to the uni, I've managed to catch up on work. But, I dunno, I feel really tired and a bit fed up," sighs Charlie.

"Listen, it was nice of Maria to visit you, but I do think you ignoring her is best. She does have this awful reputation for being a player. Like I said, I saw her with that blonde in The Unicorn, on Saturday, and when she saw me she looked sheepish, as if she had been caught out or something. No, she's bad news. You are better off without her."

Stella helps Charlie pack the last few things from her room. After Christmas, she will be moving into the bungalow that Brenda owns, and she can't wait to get there. She is happy that Stella is moving in with her. She is such a good friend, and Charlie knows she needs people she trusts, around her. They head into town with a few things for charity shops, and as they pass Costello's, they see someone crouched on the floor, head in hands, next to a bucket and scrubbing brush. As they get closer the figure looks up at them.

"Maria, what's happened? Are you okay?" shouts Charlie.

"I'm okay. Go on, you can't help me, I'll be fine. Some homophobic idiots threw a brick through my window and sprayed graffiti all over the door. Look, the idiots can't even spell dyke properly. Must be kids."

Charlie and Stella help Maria off the floor.

"I'm so sorry," says Charlie. "Will you be okay?"

"Well, luckily the restaurant has been doing well, so I can afford the repairs. But god knows what this has done for business. I know this is Brighton, but some of the older generation campaign hard against gay rights, so this could really do some damage." Maria shrugs. "Hey, I can't change everyone's opinion, can I?"

Stella picks up the brush and tries to scrub the paint from the pavement.

"Listen, I'm sorry," says Charlie, "I am leaving for home in the morning, for Christmas break, but let's meet for a drink when I get back, okay? Text me if you want. I am sorry this has happened. Did you report it to the police?"

"No point. They have more important things to do. No, I'll just clean up the mess and think of a way to salvage my reputation. You have a nice Christmas, okay? How's your back now? All good?"

"Yes, I'm fine, thanks. Listen, I've got to go, but I'll text you, okay? Take care, Maria."

"Never seen her look so upset," says Stella, as they walk into the charity shop.

"So, now what do I do?" asks Charlie.

"Nothing. You are being strong, remember?"

As they walk home, Charlie can't get Maria's look of sadness out of her mind. Then she gets a text: What time are you getting the train tomorrow? I would like to say goodbye properly. Give me a chance to explain a few things before you go. If you don't reply I know it's a no, and I won't bother you again. Luv M xx

"Oh god, Stella, it's Maria. She wants to meet me before I go tomorrow. What shall I do?"

"I wouldn't give in, or give her the satisfaction of your time, after she did that to you. She's a player, and always will be, road runner. Don't get hurt by her twice!"

Chapter 11

Charlie is finishing last minute packing and making sure she has all the presents. It wouldn't go down well if she forgot any. She hears her phone ring, but it stops before she gets to it, then a text comes through: What time is your train? I really need to see you.

Charlie replies: I'll be there from ten a.m. My train is just after eleven.

As she arrives by taxi, she sees Maria by the ticket office, looking at her watch. They greet each other awkwardly and after Charlie gets her ticket and lets the staff know she needs assistance, the pair make their way up to the coffee shop next to the platforms.

"I haven't always been like this, you know," announces Maria.

"How do you mean? Like what?"

"I have a reputation with the ladies. You may have heard."

"Yes, I had heard. So why are you telling me this? What do I care? You got what you wanted and left, didn't you?"

"Ouch! I guess I deserved that. Listen, there's a lot about me you don't know, okay? And an hour in a train station isn't long enough to explain. But please know, I am sorry, and I do really care about you. Okay? I've changed ... for the better, and you have helped me do that, so thanks. Listen, I have written you a letter explaining things. Old fashioned, I know, but you need to know the truth. Please read it when you are away, and if you want to meet up in the New Year, I will be waiting to hear from you. Please, Charlie, don't be angry with me. I ..."

"What?"

"I think I love you, okay? But we need to talk. I just need you to know I'm genuine and that I want us to be together."

Wow! Charlie can't quite take in what she just heard from Maria's lips ... she loves me? But Charlie knows she needs to keep her dignity and stay calm.

"That came from nowhere," laughs Charlie. "Okay, I'm not taking the piss, sorry, I'm just a bit shocked. Give me the letter; I'll read it and we can talk soon. No promises, but let's get Christmas over with, then meet up."

They drink coffee and eat muffins.

"These are not as good as the ones you made me," smiles Charlie.

"You do have quite an appetite, don't you? In a morning, I mean." Maria gives Charlie a longing look, but this time with tears in her eyes. She takes Charlie's hand and whispers, "I need you, Charlie, just read the letter please, my love. You have shown me how to love; don't leave me now."

It is time to leave. The station staff member comes to collect Charlie, the pair say an awkward goodbye, and Charlie is on her way. She looks out of the window and sees Maria on the platform.

"Call me," Maria gestures, as the train pulls away.

Chapter 12

Christmas in the Duke house is no different this year from any other, except Charlie knows she can escape soon after. Her mum always buys less than useless gifts and the hand-made ones are usually even worse.

The only great thing is the food. They always go overboard on food and sweets. Charlie enjoys this indulgence. Meal times are frustrating now, as her mum constantly makes remarks about Charlie not eating enough veg or else drinking too much alcohol. Charlie always finds a funny remark to answer her mum with, even when seriously annoyed. She never pushes the drinking thing though, because she knows it is a sore subject. Dave - always on her side in an argument - is her stepdad. Charlie's real dad died from a drink-related illness when she was little.

Charlie likes to tease her younger sister, Dylan, saying she only ever comes out of her bedroom for Christmas and is never seen after that. There is a nine year age difference between the two, but this Christmas, Dylan seems to have grown up a bit and is dressing quite butch. Is she gay? wonders Charlie.

Brighton is a real mixture at this time of year: lots of visitors on Christmas party trips, bright lights and live music in the streets, kids running around on the beach with their new bikes, and couples walking arm in arm on the pier. On the other side of town, though, the atmosphere is very different. Sitting in darkness, watching TV and drinking a bottle of vintage scotch, a sad figure reflects on a recent past mostly thrust upon her shoulders. Having had to move miles away to run the family business after her uncle died, no real friends and definitely no girlfriend, Maria in private is a very different character to the one projected onto the outside world. Yes, she has a nice house, a business which is doing quite well in spite of the recession, and lots of women willing to leave their husbands, boyfriends and girlfriends for her, but something is missing. She remembers being bullied at school for looking very different from a young age.

"Are you a boy, or a girl?" they would tease. "They came over from Italy, her family, you know. Maybe they are part of the Mafia and she's running away," they would say. Mafia Kid was her nickname.

Her family, especially her proud Italian father, never accepted her sexuality. Being a lesbian wasn't the right way to live your life.

"You are a woman and you should have a husband and many children," her dad protested, when she came out. She tried to live the straight life as a teenager, but never felt comfortable being who they wanted her to be. The night her uncle Vinnie raped her, still gave her nightmares. They got her drunk on her eighteenth birthday and started to mess around with her - all four uncles and a few of the cousins too. She was blind drunk, and powerless to defend herself. Her birthday is on New Year's Eve, so tonight is one hell of an anniversary. She finishes the bottle of scotch by eleven p.m. and gets ready for bed. She intends to go into work tomorrow, to stock take and do some new menus, so she wants an early night. She stumbles into bed and starts to dream of being in a safe, warm place, with bright colours and sunshine. Yes, she is dreaming about Charlie. She misses Charlie. She loves Charlie.

Chapter 13

New Year's Day starts slowly at the Duke residence. They all get up, shower and dress around eleven, trying on an array of new clothes and spraying themselves with new perfumes. Linda looks over the instruction manual of her new bread maker and Dylan helps make some dough for a loaf, to go in after lunch. They decide to go for a walk in the fields behind their bungalow, but Charlie wants to stay in the warm. Besides, the football is on and she wants to watch the game. Dave also wants to watch the game, but goes along to keep the peace. Charlie retreats into her room to try on some new clothes, and sits on the bed for a minute. She feels something underneath her and pulls out a piece of paper from under the duvet ... Maria's letter.

Dear Charlie

A letter from the heart, from me to you.

I know sometimes the world seems such a bitter place, feels like you've reached the end of every road. Well, I've been walking down this avenue for such a long time, and I find myself standing here, outside your door.

You opened up and let me into your world and I got lost there for a while. You showed me how to laugh, to play, to be free; showed me compassion, unconditionally. But the best thing

that you gave me, I will never forget.
You showed me how to love.

The letter explains in detail what happened to Maria on the night of the rape and how she had found it hard to commit to relationships since. By sleeping around, she could keep people out so she didn't get hurt.

If she ever did let anyone in, she would never be able to take that person home to meet her family, as the person would be a woman and that would never be accepted. So, the letter explains, it is easier to stay single ...

I know that's the coward's way to live a life, but I've never found anyone to snap me out of it – to make me appreciate real love... until now, Charlie. You opened my eyes to a whole different world: the problems you face every day of your life, all the stares and the physical challenges. And you always have a smile, and you always ask how someone is, before you talk about how you are. You show compassion to those less fortunate than yourself; you forgive and forget; and I've never seen you cry, even when I treated you so badly after our first night together.

I did carry on with my old ways, and I did chat up other women in the pub. Not because I wanted to be with them, but because I was afraid to be me; afraid to let my guard down and really feel for someone. But each time I tried it on with another woman, all I could think of was holding you, Charlie. I wasn't being harsh towards women; I was scared to love, until you came along. You took my hand and told me it would be okay.

You showed me how to love, now let me love you, too. Come back to me and I will give you my all and make you happy. Just say you will stay with me.

Chapter 14

Before she knows it, term has started. Now, life is pretty much back to normal, except she is living out of boxes, as she still has things to unpack at the bungalow.

Charlie is in a panic because, in her wisdom, Stella has arranged a house warming party tonight. During the two weeks she has been back in Brighton, things have improved. Uni is going well; she is getting great marks, making friends and going out lots. Her confidence is high. She has even met a few ladies, joined a dating agency and had a few dates.

The bungalow is as good as it is going to get tonight, and guests start to arrive.

Delta turns up with Brenda in tow. Those two are not a couple yet, but by now Charlie can see Brenda is completely in love with Delta.

Rachel, from Delta's social group, who Charlie is kind of seeing now, arrives next. Rachel is quite a handful, a bit rebellious at uni, but great fun. They had very exciting sex to begin with, but Charlie doesn't have deep feelings for her. Halfway through the evening, the pair disappear and have sex: wild, sweaty sex, but it is just sex and she knows there has to be more. They have a row shortly after, when Charlie suggests Rachel has had enough to drink. When she tries to take a bottle from her, Rachel kicks off, storms out and disappears.

Charlie pours herself a drink and turns the music up even louder than before. She is now definitely in party mood. Over the music she hears a few load bangs, after which Delta comes out of the bathroom followed by a very sheepish looking Brenda. The whole place gives a huge roar: there is clapping and wolf whistling.

"There we have proof," says Stella. "Those too are fucking now, even if they weren't before."

"If you can't beat em, join em, kid," says Delta.

"It's only been on the cards for about twenty years," says Brenda, proudly.

The party is in full swing by now and everyone is very hyper and seems to be enjoying themselves. But Charlie sits for a minute, in the kitchen, looking at her phone.

"For god's sake, Charlie, ring her," says Stella. "You've been back weeks now. We all know how you feel, so ..."

Charlie jumps as the phone rings. It is Maria.

"Hey, it's me. I heard you were having a party. I have a house warming gift for you. Can I come over?"

There is a long pause.

"Charlie, we need to talk. Please let me see you. If you don't want to know me after we talk, you will never see me again, I promise."

"... Okay." She gives Maria the address and tells her to bring a bottle. "We are running low here, are we not, girls?"

"Yaaaaaa."

"Yes, bring a bottle, Maria, and for god's sake, Charlie, put the woman out of her misery!" shouts Stella.

"Shhhhhhhhh, Stella!" snaps Charlie.

By the time Maria arrives, most of the party have left. Delta and Brenda are being cute in the corner, like a couple of kids. Maria walks in shyly, looking around to see who is in the room.

"So, you're the mystery women that's taken the focus of my star student."

"Shhhhhhhhh, D, don't embarrass the poor woman," scolds Brenda.

"Shouldn't we be going, honey? It's a school night for me. It's a free study period in the morning, Charlie, so I'll see you at one thirty, okay? New assignment for you, so be ready."

"Come on, D, you're wasted. I gotta get you home."

"Now there's an offer I've been waiting for all these years. He he," giggles Delta.

"Oi, come on woman; leave these two to talk."

Brenda struggles to get a very drunk Delta from the sofa to her chair. Maria goes over to help.

"You've carried someone from their chair before, then, gal?"

"Yes, I have had some experience of that, Delta. It is nice to meet you. We must talk. I have a business idea you may be able to help me out with."

"Sure, honey, let's have a beer in The Unicorn one time. Right now, I gotta sleep. The room's kinda spinning, you know."

Everyone giggles.

"Goodnight, you two, and thanks for coming tonight," says Charlie, smiling as she proudly looks around her new home.

After they leave, Charlie goes to the kitchen to make coffee.

"You want one?" she asks Maria.

"I got something a lot stronger. You fancy a drink?" Maria holds up a bottle of scotch.

"Now, the last time you offered me a scotch, look what happened. You got me in all kinds of trouble." Charlie flashes Maria that childlike cheeky look of hers.

"Yeah, and you loved every second of it, didn't you, sweetheart?" At this, Maria straddles herself on Charlie's lap and they embrace. "I'm holding you now and I am never letting you go again." They kiss passionately.

"Have you really changed, Maria? Can you be with the same person for a long time without being unfaithful?" asks Charlie.

"Hey, I've got a business, a house, and I'm successful, but you are the one who taught me how to love."

With this, Maria carries Charlie into the bedroom and lays her on the bed. Slowly and carefully she undresses Charlie and then removes her own clothes, too. Charlie looks at Maria's beautiful body, then deep into those baby blue eyes. But this time it is different; she can see the two of them being happy together. And she really doesn't care who taught who how to love.